*I would like to formally thank Maddy for the wolves and Liam for the pig-puppet. I would like to dedicate this book to Chiara, who could scare away a hundred wolves, and to Tash, who could give them her spaghetti Bolognese.*
—Neil Gaiman

*This book is for my son Liam, as a small thank you for loaning me his special Pig Number 1 for the photographs included herein. Stunt pig number 2 was also useful, but the presence of pig-the-original on set was a true privilege.*
—Dave McKean

STRAWBERRY

JAM    454g

# THE WOLV

BLOOMSBURY
CHILDREN'S
BOOKS

First published in Great Britain in 2003 by
Bloomsbury Publishing Plc
38 Soho Square, London, W1D 3HB

First published in the US by
HarperCollins Publishers

Text copyright © 2003 Neil Gaiman
Illustrations copyright © 2003 Dave McKean
The moral rights of the author and illustrator
have been asserted

A CIP catalogue record of this book is available
from the British Library
ISBN 0 7475 6953 3

Printed in China

10 9 8 7 6 5 4

# VES IN THE WALLS

WRITTEN BY
NEIL GAIMAN

ILLUSTRATED BY
DAVE MᶜKEAN

BLOOMSBURY

**Lucy** walked around the house.

Inside the house everything was quiet.
Her mother was putting homemade
**jam** into pots.

Her father was out at his job,
playing the **tuba**.

Her brother was in the living
room playing **video games**.

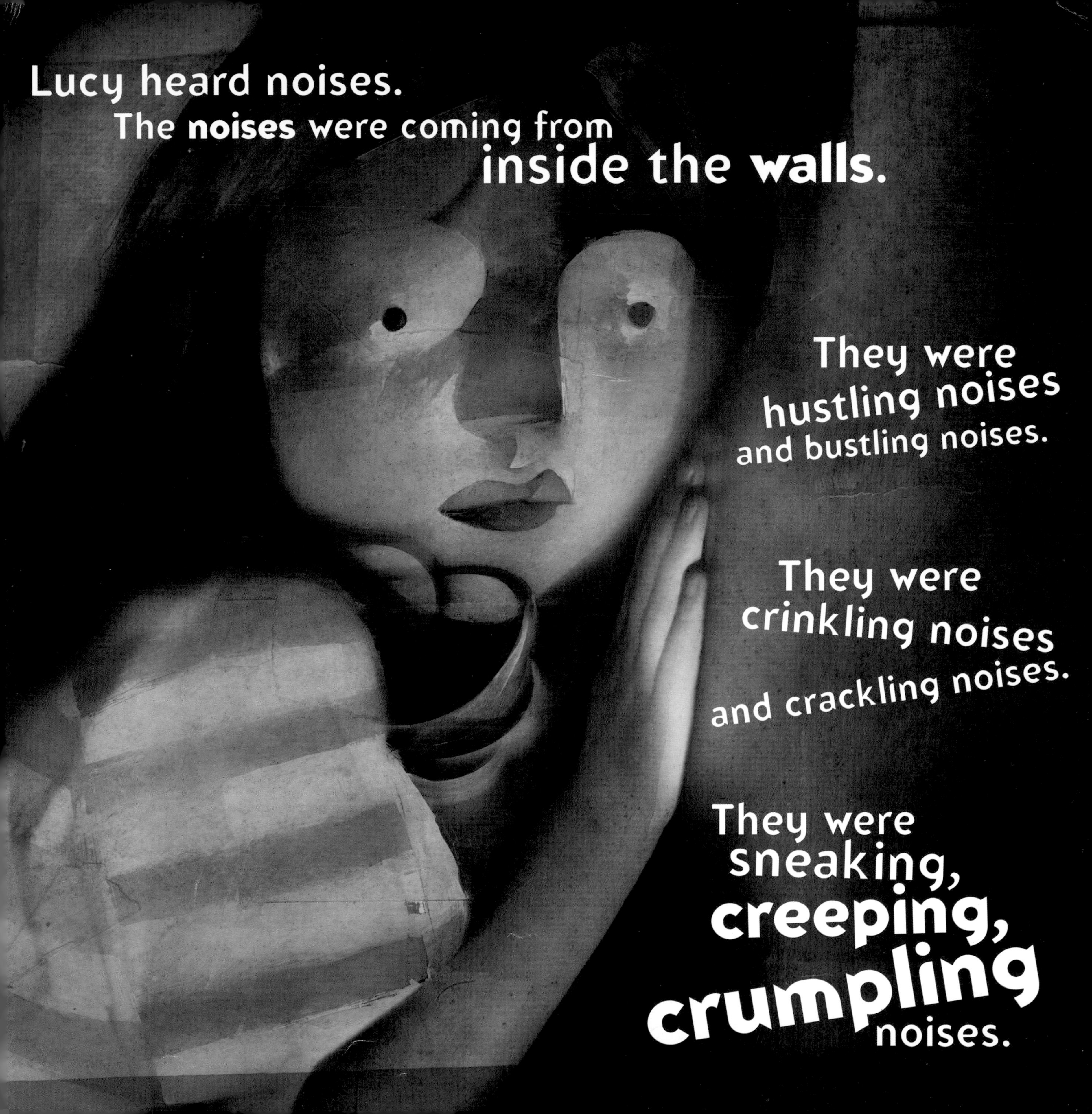

Lucy heard noises.
The **noises** were coming from
inside the **walls.**

They were
hustling noises
and bustling noises.

They were
crinkling noises
and crackling noises.

They were
sneaking,
**creeping,**
**crumpling**
noises.

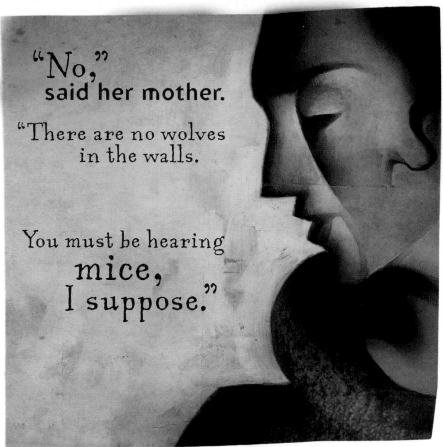

"No,"
said her mother.

"There are no wolves
in the walls.

You must be hearing
mice,
I suppose."

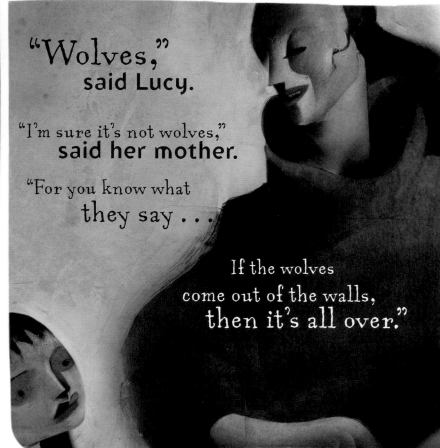

"Wolves,"
said Lucy.

"I'm sure it's not wolves,"
said her mother.

"For you know what
they say . . .

If the wolves
come out of the walls,
then it's all over."

"What's
all over?"
asked Lucy.

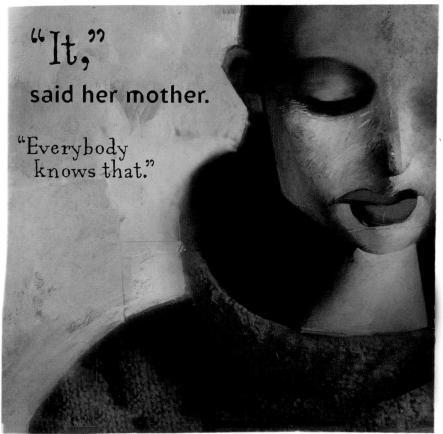

"It,"
said her mother.

"Everybody
knows that."

Lucy picked up her pig-puppet doll, which she'd had since she was a little, little baby.

"I don't think it sounds like mice,"

she said to her pig-puppet.

In the middle of the night when everything was still, she heard **clawing** and **gnawing**, **nibbling** and **squabbling.**
She could hear the wolves in the walls, plotting their wolfish plots, hatching their wolfish schemes.

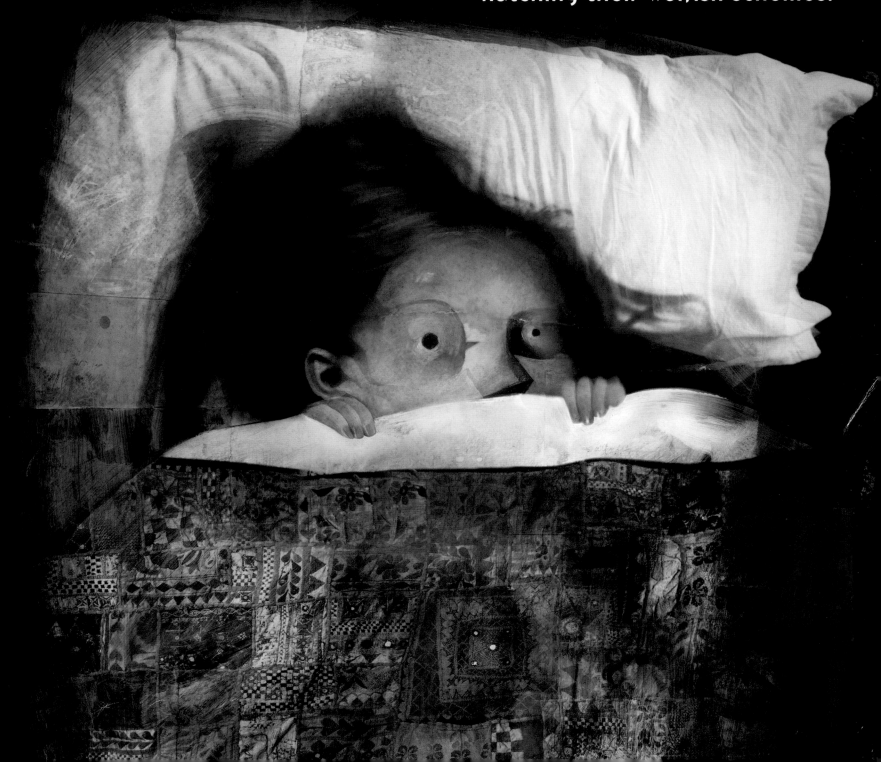

In the day,
Lucy felt eyes upon her,
watching her from the cracks
and from the holes in the walls.

They peeped through the eyes
in paintings.

She went to talk to her father.

"There are wolves
in the walls,"
she told him.

"I don't think there are, poppet," **he told her.** "You have an overactive imagination.

Perhaps the noises you heard come from rats. Sometimes you get rats in big old houses like this."

"It's wolves," said Lucy.

"I can feel them in my tummy.

And pig-puppet thinks it's wolves as well."

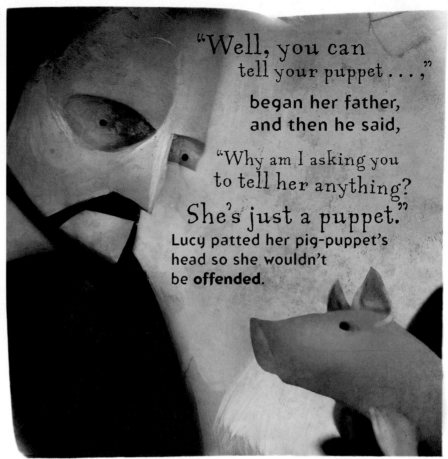

"Well, you can tell your puppet . . . ," began her father, and then he said,

"Why am I asking you to tell her anything? She's just a puppet." Lucy patted her pig-puppet's head so she wouldn't be **offended.**

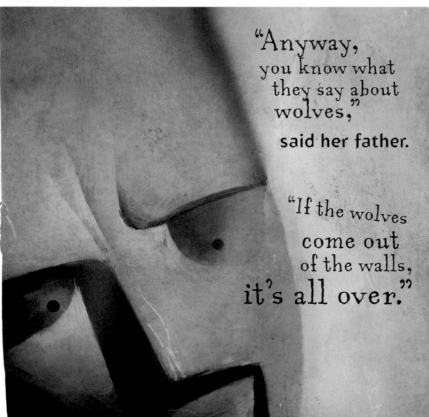

"Anyway, you know what they say about wolves," said her father.

"If the wolves come out of the walls, it's all over."

"Who says that?" **asked Lucy.**

"People. Everybody. You know," said her father,

and he went back to practicing his tuba.

She was drawing a picture when she heard the noises **again,**

a scrambling,
**rambling,**
**rustling**
in the walls.

"There are wolves
in the walls,"
she told her brother.

"Bats,"
he said.

"You think it's bats?" she asked.

"No," he said. "I think *you* are!"

And he laughed for a long time at his own joke, although it had not been a particularly good one.

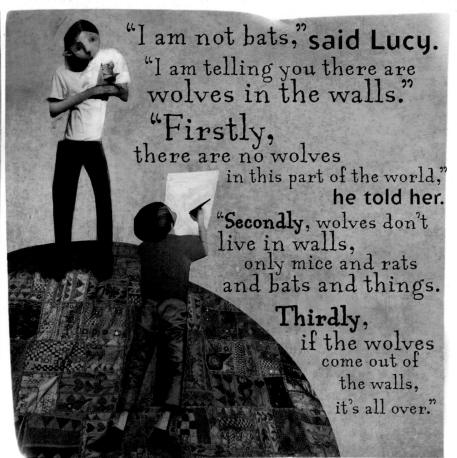

"I am not bats," said Lucy. "I am telling you there are wolves in the walls."

"Firstly, there are no wolves in this part of the world," he told her. "Secondly, wolves don't live in walls, only mice and rats and bats and things.

Thirdly, if the wolves come out of the walls, it's all over."

"Who says?" asked Lucy.

"Mister Wilson at my school," said her brother.

"He teaches us about wolves and things."

"And how does *he* know?" asked Lucy.

"Everybody knows," said her brother, and he went back to doing his homework.

The next day the noises were louder.

"We have to do something about those mice,"

said her mother.

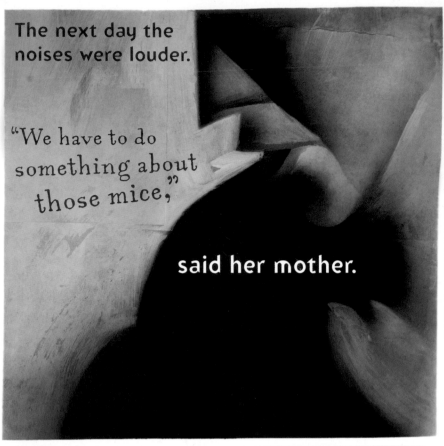

"Pesky rats!"

said her father.

"I'll call someone up about them in the morning."

"It's bats, I know it is!" said her brother, happily.

"I shall ensure that I sleep with my neck exposed tonight, in case one of them is a vampire bat. Then, if it bites me I shall be able to fly and sleep in a coffin, and never have to go to school in the daytime again."

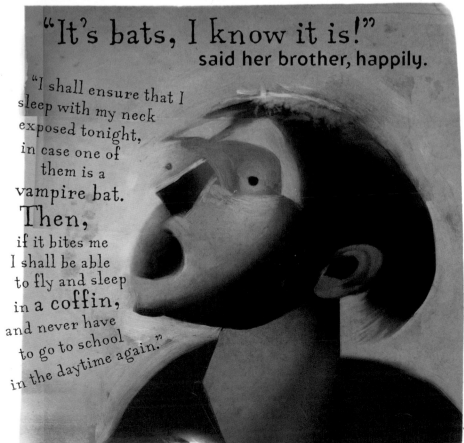

But Lucy did not think it was mice or rats or bats. She shook her head at this sad display of ignorance. Then she cleaned her teeth, and she kissed her mother and father, and she took herself off to her bed.

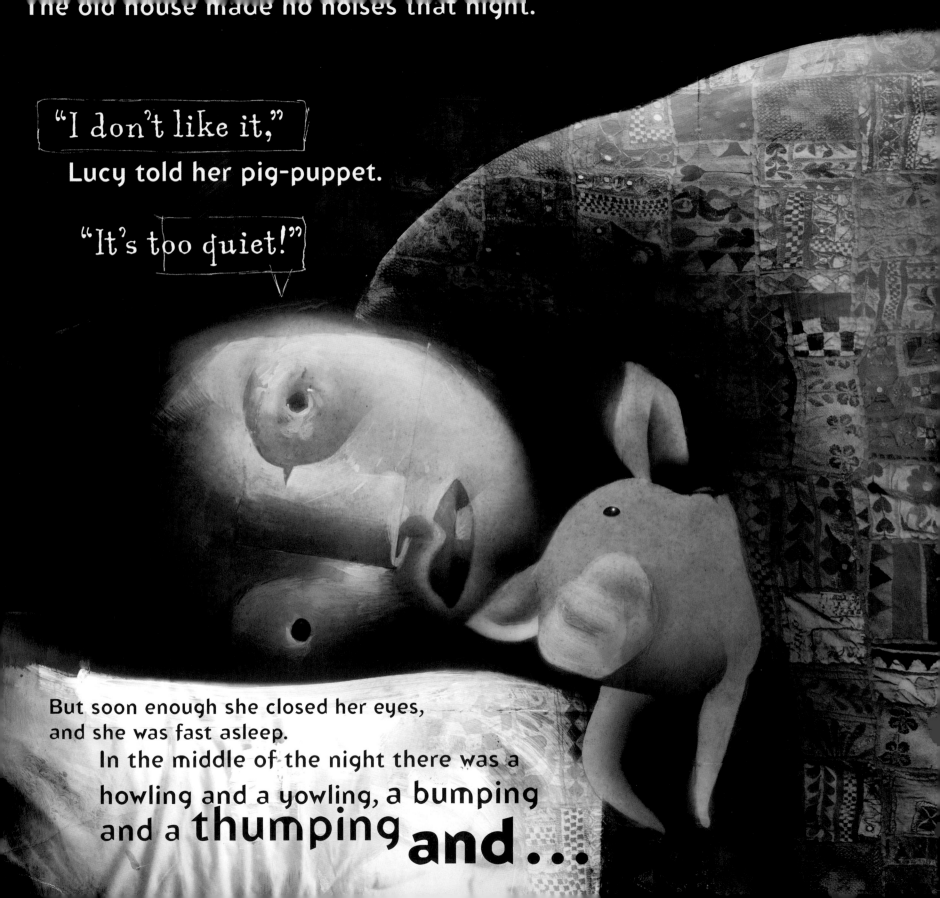

The old house made no noises that night.

"I don't like it,"
Lucy told her pig-puppet.

"It's too quiet!"

But soon enough she closed her eyes,
and she was fast asleep.
In the middle of the night there was a
howling and a yowling, a bumping
and a **thumping** and...

...the **wolves** came out of the **walls**.

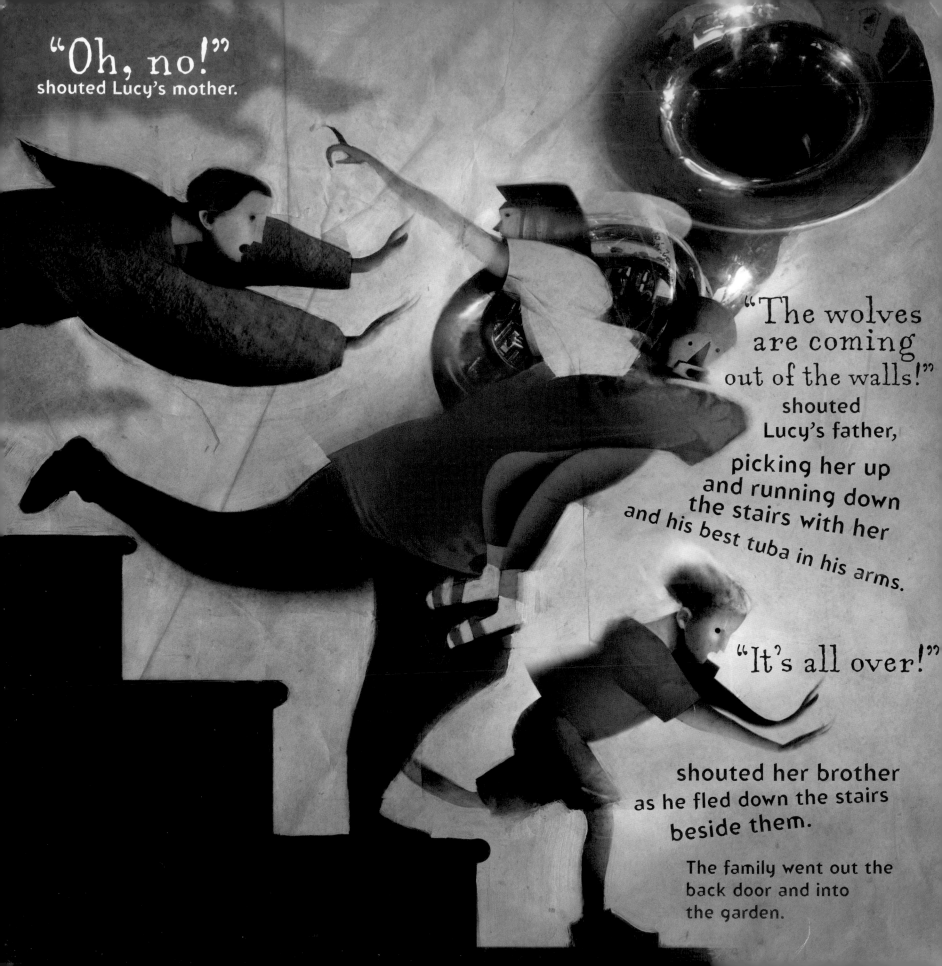

They huddled at the bottom
of the garden that night.

The lights were on in every room of their house.
Back in the house they knew the wolves were watching their
television and eating the food from the family's pantry and
dancing wolfish dances up the stairs and down again.

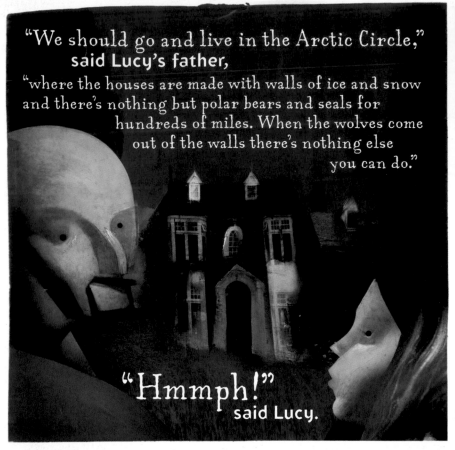

"We should go and live in the Arctic Circle," said Lucy's father, "where the houses are made with walls of ice and snow and there's nothing but polar bears and seals for hundreds of miles. When the wolves come out of the walls there's nothing else you can do."

"Hmmph!" said Lucy.

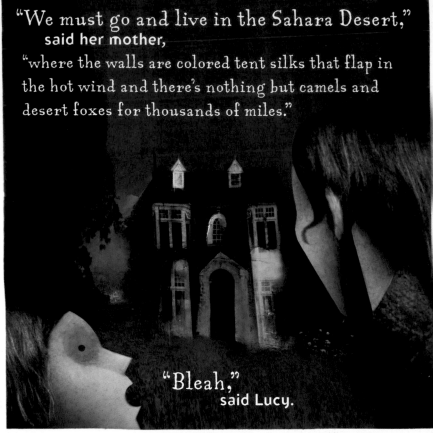

"We must go and live in the Sahara Desert," said her mother, "where the walls are colored tent silks that flap in the hot wind and there's nothing but camels and desert foxes for thousands of miles."

"Bleah," said Lucy.

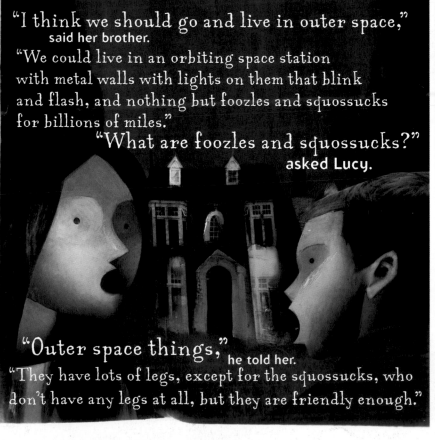

"I think we should go and live in outer space," said her brother. "We could live in an orbiting space station with metal walls with lights on them that blink and flash, and nothing but foozles and squossucks for billions of miles."

"What are foozles and squossucks?" asked Lucy.

"Outer space things," he told her. "They have lots of legs, except for the squossucks, who don't have any legs at all, but they are friendly enough."

"I don't want to live anywhere that isn't my house," said Lucy. "And I've left my pig-puppet behind!"

"We can get you a new one, wherever we're going," said her mother.

"Now, let's try to go to sleep."

It was chilly at the
bottom of the garden,
and Lucy missed her
**pig-puppet.**

"She'll be all alone in that
house with the wolves,"
she thought.

"They could do dreadful
things to her."

So Lucy crept back
up the garden,
quieter than any
mouse, and she
slipped up the back
steps, and through
the back door, and
into the house.

Lucy was standing there,
in the little hall at the back
of the house, when she
heard some wolves coming
down the stairs.
They had been eating
jam and toast in front
of the television,
and were coming
back for more.

Where could she go?
What could she do?

Quick as the
**flick**
of the **wing**
of a bat,

Lucy slipped into the wall.

She crept through the house
on the inside,

through the downstairs,

up the middle

and into the wall of her bedroom.

There was a **huge wolf**,
fat as **anything**,
asleep on her bed.
He was wearing her socks:
two on his back paws, one on his ear,
and one on the tip of his tail.

He was snoring **very loudly**.

Lucy pushed open
the picture that

hung over her bed
and she **climbed down—**

**carefully—**

quietly—

and she picked up
her **pig-puppet**
from the floor

and gave
her a hug.

"Snorgle snurk,"
snored the wolf, fast asleep.

Quiet as a shadow,
Lucy climbed up to the
top of her old doll's house,
and from there to the
top of a chest of drawers,
and from there to the mantelpiece,
and behind the picture
and back into the walls.

"It's kind of nice
in the walls,"
she thought.

"I was worried sick about you!"
she told her pig-puppet,

and she **squeezed** her very tightly.

Through the walls crept Lucy,
and back into the garden.

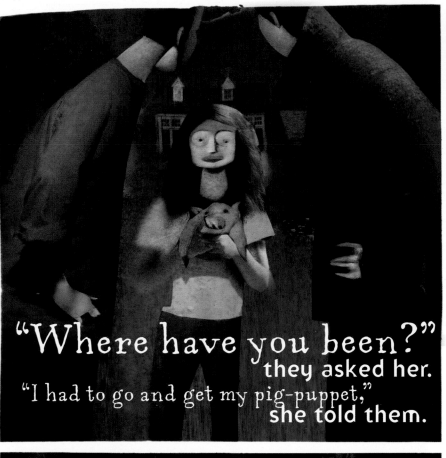

"Where have you been?" they asked her.
"I had to go and get my pig-puppet," she told them.

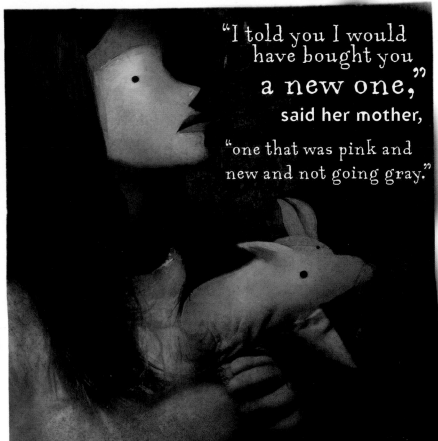

"I told you I would have bought you a new one," said her mother, "one that was pink and new and not going gray."

"That was why I went back to get my pig-puppet," said Lucy.

And she went back to sleep, cuddling her pig.

The next morning,
  Lucy's mother went to work,
  and Lucy's brother went to school,
  and Lucy and her father sat down at the
  bottom of the garden.
    He practiced his tuba,
    and read travel brochures.

"We could go and live on a desert island," her father told them all that evening (over a dinner of hamburgers and french fries and little apple-pies with astonishingly hot middles which Lucy's mother had brought for them when she got back from work). "We could live in a grass hut with grass walls on an island in the middle of the sea, with nothing but goats on the island and nothing but fishes in the sea."

"We could live in a hot-air balloon," said her mother.

"We could live in a tree-house at the top of a very tall tree," said her brother.

"Or we could go back and live in our house again," said Lucy.

"What?"
said her
father.

"What?"
said her
mother.

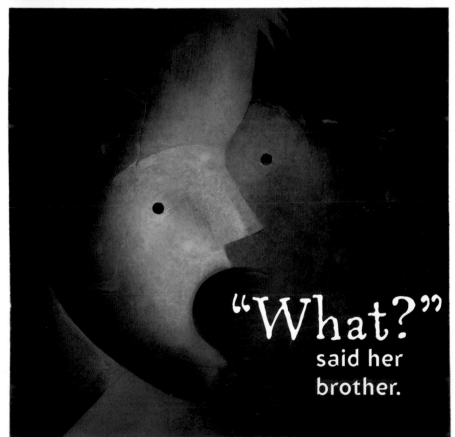

"What?"
said her
brother.

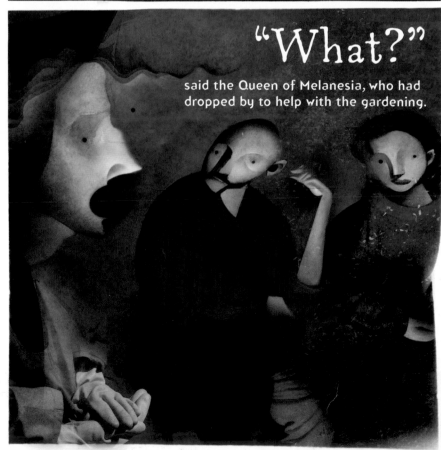

"What?"
said the Queen of Melanesia, who had dropped by to help with the gardening.

"Well," said Lucy, "there's a lot of space in the walls of the house.

And at least it isn't cold there."

"What about the wolves?" asked her father.

"They are in the house," said Lucy.

"Not the walls."

Lucy's mother and father and brother grumbled and frowned. Still, none of them wanted to spend another night sleeping at the bottom of the garden.

They tried sleeping in the shed,
but it smelled too much of
lawnmowers and of the
fertilizer used for the rhubarb.

So they crept up the back steps ...

Through the back door—

into the back hall—

and into the walls.

"We must be very quiet," said Lucy.

But the wolves were making such a noise that no one could have heard them anyway.

The family crept through the walls of the house, peeking out through the eye-holes of paintings and through the cracks of things.

There were wolves watching television
and eating popcorn.

They had turned the
television up as **loud**
as it would go,

and they had spilled popcorn
all over the floor,
where it stuck to the
unfinished slices of toast and jam.

There were wolves **dashing** up the stairs.

There were wolves **sliding** down the banisters.

Some of the wolves had put on the family's nicest clothes, and they had made big holes in the back of them, for their tails.

The family went to sleep in the walls.

In the middle of the night something woke them up.

The Wolves

One of the wolves was playing
her brother's video game,
and was beating all
the high scores.

The biggest,
**fattest** wolf of all
was playing
an old wolf
melody on
Lucy's father's
second-best
tuba.

"My jam!
My walls!"
said Lucy's mother.

"My video game high scores!"
said Lucy's brother.

"My second-best tuba!"
said Lucy's father.

"Right.
I've had enough,"
said Lucy.

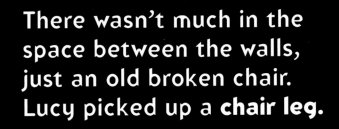

There wasn't much in the
space between the walls,
just an old broken chair.
Lucy picked up a **chair leg.**

"You know,
I've had just about as
much as I can take of
those wolves too,"
said her father,
and her mother,
and her brother.

Each of her family picked up a broken chair leg.

"Ready?" said her mother.
"Ready," said everybody else.

And . . .

Round and around they ran, gathering up their most treasured possessions.

"Flee!" they shouted.

"Flee! Flee! Flee! For once the people come out of the walls, it's all over!"

Down the stairs went the wolves, scurrying and hurrying and tumbling over each other in their hurry to get out of the house and get away

And the wolves **ran** and they **ran** and they **ran** and they **ran** and they didn't stop running until they got somewhere where there would never be any people in the walls who would come out in the middle of the night **whooping** and **singing** people songs and brandishing chair legs.

And whether they went to the Arctic or the desert or outer space, or somewhere else entirely, nobody knows.

**But from that day to this, those wolves have never again been seen.**

It took the family **several days** of cleaning up to make the house look anything like it did before the **wolves** came out of the **walls.**

But eventually everything was back the way it had been before, except for Lucy's father's second-best tuba, which had sustained severe jam damage.

So Lucy's father sold his second-best tuba and bought a sousaphone instead, which he had always wanted.

And everything went back to normal....

**Until** Lucy noticed something funny.

She heard rustlings and scratchings and squeezings and creakings in the old house, and then, one night ...

... she heard a noise that sounded exactly like an **elephant trying not to sneeze.**

She went and got her pig-puppet.

"Do you think I should tell the rest of them," she said,

"that we have elephants living in the walls of our house?"

And they did.